# RAY CHARLES

*Illustrated by Meryl Henderson*

# RAY CHARLES
*Young Musician*

*by Susan Sloate*

## ALADDIN PAPERBACKS

New York   London   Toronto   Sydney

This book is a work of fiction. Any references to historical events, real people,
or real locales are used fictitiously. Other names, characters, places, and
incidents are the product of the author's imagination, and any resemblance to
actual events or locales or persons, living or dead, is entirely coincidental.

ALADDIN PAPERBACKS
An imprint of Simon & Schuster
Children's Publishing Division
1230 Avenue of the Americas
New York, NY 10020
Text copyright © 2007 by Susan Sloate
Illustrations copyright © 2007 by Meryl Henderson
All rights reserved, including the right of
reproduction in whole or in part in any form.
ALADDIN PAPERBACKS, CHILDHOOD OF FAMOUS AMERICANS,
and colophon are trademarks of Simon & Schuster, Inc.
Designed by Lisa Vega
The text of this book was set in New Caledonia.
Manufactured in the United States of America
First Aladdin Paperbacks edition January 2007
2  4  6  8  10  9  7  5  3  1
Library of Congress Control Number 2006926943
ISBN-13: 978-1-4169-1437-2
ISBN-10: 1-4169-1437-4

# ILLUSTRATIONS

# CONTENTS

# RAY CHARLES

# Musical Keys

Ray Charles Robinson was born in Georgia, just north of the Florida border, on September 23, 1930. His mama was only about sixteen years old at the time. Ray's father, Bailey, a tall, strapping man, worked on the local railroad. But he was hardly ever around, and Ray almost never saw him. He only visited once in a while.

Mama soon brought Ray to Greenville, Florida, looking for work. Ray's mama did all kinds of work, like snapping beans and shelling peas. Mostly she did laundry, washing and

1

ironing it for the town's white people. A year later, Ray's little brother, George, was born.

The town's real name was Greenville, but most people who lived there, including little Ray and his mama, 'Retha, called it Greensville, with an *s*. Perched right on the border of Florida and Georgia, it was a deep southern country town, which meant hot, sticky summers; great southern food, like barbecued ribs and grits; and an understanding, in the early 1930s, that white folks lived in one part of town and black folks lived in another. That was just the way things were.

Little Ray thought his world was just fine. He had his little brother, George, for company, his mama and stepmother, Mary Jane, to raise him and love him, and his friend Mr. Pit to teach him about music.

Mama was very strict about both chores and manners. At the top of her list were two iron-clad rules: You do not beg and you do not steal. Ray and George knew she meant them.

One day Ray finished his chores quickly. Until he and George were through picking up chips for the fire, clearing up after lunch, and making the bed, they were not allowed to go anywhere. And Ray wanted to go someplace special today: He was going to visit Mr. Pit.

Ray wiped the last of the dishes from lunch. He looked over the last plate carefully to be sure it was dry, and set it atop a stack near the sink. He hung the towel carefully over the counter to dry. Now he could go.

Outside in the yard, George, who was a year younger than Ray, looked up hopefully as Ray came through the door. He wanted to play with Ray; he had a tiny frog in his hand. He opened his hand to show it, but Ray shook his head. "Not today, George. I got somewhere to go."

George was a good playmate, and Ray usually liked to play with him, but when he visited Mr. Pit, he went alone.

Ray ran to the Red Wing Café, just a few buildings down the road. As usual he was barefoot. He and George never wore shoes. Black people in Greenville mostly didn't own shoes, and they didn't mind, either. The weather was usually warm, and their feet were used to the dirt roads. In the hot summers, they walked on the cool grass, not the blazing hot roads. Ray didn't even think about his feet today, squishing along happily in the mud from last night's rain. He just hoped Mr. Pit would be waiting for him.

The Red Wing Café was the center of life in Greenville for black folks. It was a general store, which sold food and all kinds of necessities. They also rented out a few rooms in the back if you needed a place to sleep. At night lots of people went there to dance and talk. But in the hot, sleepy summer afternoons, when just a few people came in to buy beer and ice cream, it was quiet. That was when Ray visited his best friend.

Mr. Pit's real name was Mr. Wylie Pitman, and he owned the Red Wing Café. Ray, though, always called him Mr. Pit. There were two things a the café that just fascinated Ray: a jukebox and a battered, old upright piano.

The jukebox was a machine that had records stored in it. On the outside were labeled buttons, each listing a song. When you dropped in a nickel and pushed the right button, the song you wanted to hear would play. Ray just loved that jukebox. It was stuffed full of good country-western songs, some boogie-woogie, some big band, and some jazz. Ray didn't care what it played. He sat, a chubby four-year-old, between the big speakers that boomed out the music. He soaked in every note, every word, eyes closed, humming or singing along, and rocked his little body from side to side.

Even better than the jukebox, though, was Mr. Pit's piano playing. Oh, how that man could play!

Today, as Ray drew near the café, he could

hear that upright booming. Mr. Pit was playing right now!

Ray wiped his muddy feet carefully on
the door mat, then ran inside as fast as his
little legs would move. Mr. Pit was sitting at
the piano, his strong hands moving fast on
the white and black keys, jabbing out great
chords, making such wonderful sounds. "Mr.
Pit! Mr. Pit! Here I am!" Ray shouted.

Mr. Pit smiled and moved over on the
scarred old piano bench. "Hop up, RC," he
said. Lots of people called Ray RC, the initials
of his first and middle names, or Mechanic,
because he loved to do things with his hands.
His sturdy little fingers were good at making things. They were even better, though, at
pounding those piano keys.

Ray jumped up onto the piano bench. He
loved it when Mr. Pit showed him how to
play the piano. Even more than hearing Mr.
Pit play, Ray loved to touch those wonderful
keys himself.

Today Mr. Pit showed him some new chords, using three fingers on each hand to touch six keys at once. He played them several times and told Ray their names. "That's C major and that's F major and that's D minor. Now you play 'em," he said.

Ray's little fingers tried to stretch as far Mr. Pit's big hands. They wouldn't quite reach that far . . . but he pounded the keys as hard as he could. Oh, how he loved making those musical sounds!

"That's good!" Mr. Pit said. "That's very good, sonny!" As Ray played the new chords over and over, Mr. Pit started playing something else at the lower end of the piano. Soon they were belting out something they'd just made up and shouting themselves hoarse with the joy of it.

Miss Georgia, Mr. Pit's wife, was laughing at the other end of the café. "RC, you sure can play that piano," she told Ray when they'd finally stopped.

Ray's little face glowed. He was always happy, just being with Mama and Mary Jane and playing with George, but nothing made him happier than making music with Mr. Pit. Something inside him just burst into flame whenever he heard good music.

When he got tired of playing, Mr. Pit sat him down between the speakers of the jukebox. Then he set the jukebox playing. Ray listened to country-western songs and jazz and big-band selections for a long time, till he could barely nod his head along with the music. Mr. Pit laughed and lifted him up. "I think that's all the music you can stand for today, RC," he told Ray. "You go on home now."

"I'll be back, Mr. Pit," Ray said, his dark eyes huge in his little face, his grin stretching from ear to ear.

Mr. Pit laughed again. "I know you will, Ray. And I'll be waiting."

Ray ran home. It was late, but he'd had

such a good day. In his yard, he saw George playing next to the big washtub Mama used to scrub laundry for the white people in town. "George, I'm back!" he shouted.

George interrupted before Ray could talk about Mr. Pit and the piano. "Listen to this, Ray!" he said. And he recited a long string of numbers, and then multiplied them in his head, giving the answers as fast as he could speak.

Ray shook his head. Everyone knew George was really smart. What other kid at age three could add and subtract and multiply without paper and pencil? "George, that's really good!"

"And listen to this," George said eagerly. "If Mama did washing for fifty people instead of ten and they all gave her six loads of wash a week, she'd be doing three hundred loads of wash!"

Mama came to the door, a bowl in her hand. She was small and slender, wearing an old cotton dress that she always kept very clean. The delicious smell of hot greens came to each boy's nose at the same time. "You come in now and wash up, both of you. I got plenty of hot food for you, and you look like you're hungry. And, George, I don't even want to think about doing three hundred loads of wash a week. I got enough to do with the wash I got."

The boys laughed as they went inside. George beamed as he ran his hands under the tap. "I'm pretty good at numbers, aren't I, Ray?"

Ray took his place at the tap and washed his hands carefully too. He knew Mama was going to check them before she'd let him eat. "Well, you get me on numbers, George, but don't forget, I can play the piano."

George couldn't think of anything to say to that. So they sat down at the kitchen table for supper.

# Disturbing Questions

A few weeks later the sun was slipping lower in the summer sky when Ray heard his friend Johnny's mother call out. "Johnny! You get in here! Supper's almost ready, and your daddy's home!"

Johnny reluctantly dropped the ball he and Ray had been throwing. "Gotta go."

"See ya tomorrow," Ray called after him. "Maybe we can play some more baseball."

"Yeah. Maybe." Johnny trotted off down the dusty road without a backward glance.

George, as usual, was dreaming of numbers. Ray could tell because George's lips were moving silently, so he must have been adding some numbers together in his head. But when Johnny went off, George came to stand beside Ray on his chubby, roly-poly legs. "Ray, tell me somethin'."

"Yeah, George?"

"Well, Johnny's daddy comes home for supper, and Wilbur's daddy comes home for supper, and them twins down the road, *their* daddy comes home for supper. How come our daddy don't come home for supper every night?"

"You know why. 'Cause our daddy works on the railroad. He can't come home much."

"But Wilbur's daddy works on the railroad. He told me so," George persisted as Ray picked up the baseball and the long stick they used for a bat and brought them into the front yard of their house. "And he *still* comes home for supper every night. Do you think our daddy doesn't like Mama's cooking?"

"That's crazy, George." Ray quickened his pace. "He'd have to love Mama's cooking. She's the best cook in town." As they reached the front steps of the porch, they could smell the good scent of Mama's country cooking. Ray sniffed in deeply. It smelled like pork, and Ray loved pork. Mama cooked all the parts of the pig, and it always tasted so good!

Ray hoped George would forget his question, but George never forgot anything. Sometimes it wasn't easy having such a smart kid for a brother. When the boys slid into their places at the table, Mama set down a steaming platter of meat.

Ray knew better than to reach for it. They had to say grace before anyone got to eat. Mama was strict about things like that. She made them go to church every single Sunday and listen to what the preacher said. She told them it would make them grow up into what she called good, upstanding men. Ray wanted to be a good man for Mama, so he listened.

But he was a little confused, too, about this subject George had raised.

Tonight Mary Jane had joined them for supper. In fact, she ate supper with them most nights, and Ray and George called her "Mother," to distinguish her from Mama. Mary Jane was Bailey's second wife and therefore the boys' stepmother, so "Mother" actually did fit. And Mama and Mary Jane always got along really well.

Mary Jane dished up the food for them, making sure to give them big portions of the steaming corn and hot greens along with the pork. As she was setting down Ray's plate, George, who had been served first and was already eating, asked abruptly, "Mama, how come our daddy don't come home for supper with us?"

Ray saw Mama and Mary Jane exchange a look. After a moment, Mama said, "Well, George, your daddy works on the railroad, you know. He can't come home very often."

"But other kids' daddies do," George persisted. "And their daddies work on the railroad too. So why doesn't our daddy come home like they do?"

Mary Jane glanced over at Mama again. "Well, George, honey," she said carefully, "when your daddy comes home, it's not for very long, and he stays with me. But he comes over to visit you. I guess you don't remember that much, since he hasn't been back since you were real little."

George looked even more puzzled, though he kept spooning food into his mouth as he thought about this. One thing you could count on with George: He always had a good appetite.

George finished a spoonful of corn and greens, and then said to Mary Jane, "But, Mother, why does he stay with you instead of with us when he comes home? We're his boys, ain't we?"

"You sure are," Mama interrupted. "Drink

your milk, Ray. It'll make you strong. Now, George, your daddy doesn't come to stay with us when he's back from railroading because he and Mother are married to each other. And married people live together."

"Then what are we?" Ray finally asked. He was getting curious about it too.

"We're his other family," Mama said firmly. "And when he comes to town he sure does like to see you boys, see how big you're growin' and find out all you're learnin' about. And Mother is your stepmama. Not many boys are lucky enough to have two mamas, you know."

She waited to see if there were any more questions, then asked one of her own. "Now, Ray, I saw you outside with that old baseball. Where did you get it?"

"I found it, Mama. Over by the old trash dump on the other side of Mr. Pit's place."

Mama glared at him. "Ray Charles Robinson, are you telling me true?"

"Yes, Mama!" Ray knew how Mama felt about her boys stealing or lying, and he dreaded a beating from her. If she thought they'd done wrong, she would haul them outside and let them have it with a strap. She insisted they never take anything from anyone else and never tell fibs. Both boys already knew that was the worst thing they could do. Mama would never let them get away with it.

George looked up from his plate to say, "It was just an old ball, Mama. Somebody'd thrown it away. It's a little worn out, but we can still play with it. Stitchin's still okay."

"You sure you didn't take it from somewhere else? Any of the folks around here?"

Both boys shook their heads. Mama fixed a stern eye on them. "How about anyone else?"

"Like the white folks?" Ray asked.

Mama nodded.

"Gosh, Mama, we know we can't go into

their side of town. We don't, honest. Never."

"Never?" Now Mama looked more worried than stern. "Do you know what kind of trouble you could get into if you go into the white folks' side of town and steal from them?"

"Now, 'Retha, they already said they didn't," Mary Jane said gently. "If they say they didn't, then they didn't. I believe 'em. You taught 'em good."

George was still curious. "Why are you so worried about us stealing from white folks, Mama? Is that worse than stealing from black folks?"

"Stealin's stealin'," Mama said firmly. "And it's a sin no matter which way you slice it. But if you was to steal from white folks . . ." She sighed and shook her head.

Ray really wanted to know why it was worse to steal from white folks than black folks. He knew it had something to do with why people with dark skin, like him and Mama and George and Mary Jane, weren't allowed to walk freely around the white folks' side of town. It also had something to do with why Mama worked so hard doing white folks' laundry. Black folks did their own laundry. White folks could afford to pay someone else to do it. But why were they different? Why was skin color so important?

There were other differences between them too, but he really didn't understand it, and from the troubled look on Mama's face, he knew tonight wasn't a good time to ask questions.

Saying nothing, he helped clear the table and stack the battered tin dishes for washing. Then he and George went off for a bath before bed. He sat for a long time in the tin tub, looking at the dark skin rippling over his hands and arms. "It's just skin," he muttered to himself as he rubbed a thin towel hard around his wet body.

"What, Ray?"

"Nothin', George. Let's get to bed."

# Tragedy

More than a year later, Ray still spent every spare minute he could with Mr. Pit. He was learning more and more about music, learning to recognize and name chords, learning to hear certain musical styles like boogie-woogie and jazz. Mr. Pit always told him he was proud of him. "You got music in your soul, sonny, that's right, just pure music in your soul. It's a gift from the good Lord, and you gotta thank Him for it by playing good and loud."

But sometimes Mr. Pit was busy, or Mama

wanted Ray to play with George in their yard. Mary Jane, Ray's stepmother, spent a lot of time at their house as well, often making meals, washing up after them, and taking care of the boys. She worked at the sawmill right in Greenville, lifting heavy, wet boards as well as any of the men could. She wasn't as tall as them, but she was so strong!

Mama, on the other hand, for all her inner strength and rules, was small and frail. Ray couldn't remember a time when she wasn't trying to stretch out her aching back or wiggle her feet, which always hurt her. Yet she never missed a day of work, and she always had time to sit with the boys after supper to find out what they were doing and tell them stories.

Ray always thought he had two mothers, in a way. He loved Mary Jane so much, and when Mama wasn't looking, Mary Jane often slipped Ray something special to eat—a piece of candy or pie. For all her strength and muscles, she was the softhearted one.

When she was around, she never let Mama whip them, even if they'd done something they knew was wrong, something Mama usually did whip them for. And Mama would always say, "Well, all right, Mary Jane, seein' as it's you askin'. I won't whip them this time."

But Mama loved them very much too. She just felt that loving them meant raising them right. If they did get out of line, Mama punished them.

It wasn't easy raising two little boys when she had to work so hard. Mama did work for other black women who took in white people's laundry, but it wasn't easy to make a living doing laundry, especially when Mama didn't have her own laundry customers. She took laundry other black women got from their white customers, scrubbed, dried, and ironed it, then returned it to the black women for them to give to their clients as though they had done it. The black women paid Mama to do this, but never very much, and she only got the extra work that they didn't have time to do. Still, Mama worked hard and didn't complain. It was all she knew how to do. She didn't have a lot of education. Even if she had, opportunities were limited for black women in Florida in the 1930s.

Today, Ray and George were playing in the yard while Mama was scrubbing some laundry. They'd been excited and silly, running in all different directions, until she told them she was going inside so she could have some peace. She could leave the laundry soaking in the washtub for a few minutes.

Ray and George chased each other around the yard, then Ray pushed George on the swing while George had recited some more of his number equations. Now they were getting tired and bored. What should they do?

Then George had an idea. "Ray, look at me!" he called. "I'm going to fly like a bird!"

The yard looked pretty flat to Ray. He laughed. "Where are you going to fly, George?

Mama said we can't leave the yard, and there's nothing here to fly off of!"

"There is so!" George insisted. "I'll climb up on the washtub! And then I'll fly off!"

Busily his little hands grabbed at the edges of the washtub, and he pulled himself up. Ray watched for a minute, then turned away, still bored. Whatever was he going to do to make the time pass till supper? He sighed. He wasn't really hungry yet, but it sure seemed like suppertime would never come today.

Behind him, there was a splash. Ray turned around. George's little feet had slipped on the rim of the washtub, and he'd fallen in. All Ray could see was George's arms, flying up and down like a bird's. The rest of his body was underwater.

Ray waited. George was going to sit up in a minute and they'd both laugh. He looked so funny with his arms going up and down like that!

The arms kept going up and down. Ray

said, "Come on, George, come out. That's enough now."

George's arms stopped flapping like a bird. The water swayed, but there was silence. "George? George, come out!"

Ray ran over to the washtub, but he was only five and was too little to pull George out of the big washtub. He couldn't help George by himself.

So he ran into the house. "Mama! George fell into the washtub and he can't get out!" Mama would fix things. Even being so little and frail, Mama could be very strong when she needed to be.

Mama had been ironing. She stared at Ray, set down the heavy iron, and flew out of the house, over to the washtub. There was no movement in the water now. Mama moaned and plunged her arms into the washtub. She hauled the sopping child out of the washtub. "George? Oh, George!"

Water streamed down George's clothes. He

was limp. Mama tried to clear out the water and get him to breathe. She pounded on his back and breathed into his mouth, trying to get him going. She begged him to breathe, to come back to her.

It was no use. George was dead. He was four years old.

For days afterward, the neighbors helped Mama in the house. They brought pots of hot food and sat with her while she cried and cried for her lost child. They all came quietly to the funeral, dressed in their best-mended cotton dresses and pants, the women wearing their Sunday hats.

After the prayers and hymns, the minister talked about how smart George was, how he would have gone so far in life. He talked about how God must have wanted George, must have needed him badly in heaven, to take him so young.

Ray sat next to Mama, staring at the little coffin where his little brother's body lay. He was numb. How could George be dead? Why, Ray didn't remember life before George came! George was his best friend; they did almost everything together.

Mary Jane sat on Mama's other side and wept and wept. Mama didn't seem to have any tears at all now. She just stared at the coffin too, clutching Ray's little fingers in her own.

"You take care of your mama now," the neighbor women told Ray in their house after the funeral. "She needs you."

Ray tried to understand that. Mama didn't seem any different. Unlike the neighbor women, whose eyes were streaming tears, Mama wasn't crying anymore. She was very quiet and very calm. She thanked the neighbors for coming and for the wonderful food they'd brought over. It was enough to last her and Mary Jane and Ray for weeks.

But Ray wasn't crying either. He just couldn't seem to understand how George could be dead. He guessed maybe Mama was wondering the same thing, even though she didn't talk to him about it. That's why she wasn't crying; she was trying to figure it out.

Later that night, when everyone had gone and Ray was trying to get to sleep in the bed he and Mama shared, he heard a choking sound. He looked toward the hallway. The rickety door was slightly open, and he could see Mama sitting alone on the old couch, clutching her head in her small hands. He guessed something must have changed and Mama must have figured out how George could have died, because now she was crying and crying.

Ray tiptoed into the living room. The neighbors had told him to take care of her, and he guessed that meant staying with her while she cried. "Mama?" he whispered. "Mama, I'm here."

Mama didn't say a word, but she clutched him to her and moaned, and in a moment

Ray could feel her wet tears soaking into his thin shirt, more and more of them falling on his head and his face and arms. And feeling Mama's small body shaking with sobs, Ray began to feel the tears welling up in him, too. In a minute he was crying just as hard as Mama was and asking God why He had to take George.

# More Tragedy

Ray and Mama and Mary Jane slowly learned to live without George, but it took many months. Ray played by himself or with the children of their nearest neighbors. He liked the other kids just fine, and they seemed to like him, too. But he and George had been such good friends, always. It was hard not having him around. No one else was quite the same as George.

So Ray spent more time with Mr. Pit, asking for more and more piano lessons. When Mr. Pit wasn't around, Ray played by himself.

He spent a lot of time sitting in front of their house, tilting his face up to the sun. Ray liked to stare directly into the warm rays, even though his eyes got all tingly when he did. No one told him that looking at the sun for a long time could be dangerous.

A few months after George died, Ray woke up one morning and felt different. His eyes had a thick film over them. It was so heavy and thick, he could hardly open them. He tried rubbing it away, but finally he had to ask Mary Jane to help him.

Mary Jane cleaned off his eyes with a soft cloth she held under the water tap. It took some scrubbing, but finally she got his eyes cleared of all the goo that was on them. When Ray could finally open his eyes all the way, he couldn't see as clearly as usual. Things looked fuzzy, not at all the way they'd been the day before. He blinked hard several times, trying to make things clearer, but they were still blurry.

"Mama?" he said at breakfast. "Mama, I can't see real good today."

Mary Jane poured him a glass of fresh milk. "'Retha, he had some kind of gunk in his eyes. Took me ten minutes to clear it out. I never seen anything quite like it."

Mama was busy cooking grits the way country people liked them. They looked pearly white on a plate and filled you up just the way hot oatmeal would. She came over to the table, with the pan filled with hot grits. "Might be just a cold. Maybe if we just clean his eyes real good, everything'll be fine."

Ray began to eat his breakfast: grits and milk and collard greens. If Mama said it would be fine, that's the way it would be.

But the next morning the same thick paste was back. When he woke up, his eyelashes were gummed together with a filmy goo. He had to rub his eyes hard just to be able to open them at all. To make matters worse, when Mama finally cleaned all that thick stuff out of his eyes, his eyesight was fuzzy again. No matter how often he blinked, he couldn't seem to make his vision clear. He had to squint to see in the yard and lean close to everything he was passing, to make out the shapes of things.

A month went by; two months. Mama had no money for a doctor, and she wasn't even sure she could find a doctor who could tell them what was wrong. Every morning when Ray woke up, the thick paste filmed over his eyes. Every morning he had to wash it out with cold water. His vision got fuzzier and fuzzier. Soon he could hardly see at all.

Finally Mama scraped up the money to take Ray to the white doctor in town.

The understanding in Greenville was that white folks and black folks didn't mix. But if a black person was with a white person, or if they needed a doctor or the hospital, they could enter the white part of town; that was all right.

There were no black doctors in Greenville. But there was a white doctor, a good man, who took care of black folks when they needed him. So Mama took Ray to see Dr. McCloud. The doctor, she thought, could tell her what was wrong and fix it.

Dr. McCloud looked at Ray and listened to Mama explain about the film over his eyes when he woke up every day. He said to Ray, "Your mama tells me you know the names of lots of animals. Can you tell me the names of the animals on that chart?" The doctor pointed a few feet away.

Ray couldn't see nearly as well as before, but he nodded that he would try. He had to squint hard at the chart to make out anything on it. "That's a cat," he said, pointing at one object. "And next to it, that's a rabbit."

"That's fine, Ray," the doctor said. "How about the line below that? Can you tell me what those animals are?"

The next line was smaller. Ray had to

squint harder to see those objects. "Um . . . that's a-a dog," he said hesitantly. "And the next one's a—" He tried hard, but the object wasn't clear. He was silent for a minute. The doctor waited. Finally Ray said, "I don't know what that next one is. I can't see it."

"That's all right, Ray," the doctor told him. "You did fine." To Mama, he said, "I have some ointment you can put around his eyes. Put it on twice a day. It should help. But you need to come back in a few weeks so I can see how he's doing." When he saw Mama bite her lip, he added, "I won't charge you for that visit. I just want to be sure the treatment works."

Mama thanked Dr. McCloud and took the ointment he gave her. She and Ray were careful to put it on twice every day, just as the doctor had them to. If Ray ever thought Mama was going to forget the ointment, he would remind her to put it on him. He didn't really like it, but if Dr. McCloud said it would help, it would.

Problem was, it didn't seem to make much

difference. Every morning he woke up with the filmy goo over his eyes. Every day he still had to wash it out before they put on the ointment. Every day it seemed harder to see what was right in front of him.

A few weeks later, Mama took Ray back to Dr. McCloud. The doctor smiled at Ray and asked how he was doing. Ray said, "Fine, sir," but he wondered what the doctor would say when he found out the ointment wasn't getting rid of the goo over his eyes.

Ray sat very quietly while Mama told Dr. McCloud they'd used the ointment every day. "But he still has that goo," she added. "Doesn't seem to be getting any better."

"Hmm," Dr. McCloud said. "Let me take a look." He examined Ray's eyes, and then showed him the same chart Ray had looked at before. "Can you tell me the names of those animals again, Ray?" The doctor pointed to a line on the chart. "Start right there, and tell me their names."

Ray tried, but it seemed the chart was even harder to see than it had been on his last visit. Finally, hesitantly, he said, "I think that first one is a snake. And then . . . um . . . an alligator—" He looked for confirmation to the doctor, but the doctor didn't nod or shake his head. He just waited. "And that last one is . . . uh . . . a horse," Ray said finally.

"Good boy," Dr. McCloud said encouragingly. "Why don't you sit outside, Ray, and look at the comic books out there? I'd like to talk to your mama for a while."

Obediently Ray went out of the office and sat down. He picked up a comic book and held it very close to his face. Usually he liked looking at the colored strips of paper, even though he couldn't read yet. The pictures were always fun.

But it wasn't one of his good days. He could hardly make out the shapes of anything on it.

The doctor quietly closed the door to his office. Mama knew he wasn't doing that because the news was good. "Tell me what's wrong with my boy," she said.

"Well, 'Retha, I'm not quite sure what's wrong. But you tell me this started a few months ago."

"Yes, sir, a few months after George—after we lost George."

"And it's been happening every day?"

"Every day."

"And his vision is getting worse, even with the ointment."

"He can hardly see across the room anymore."

"And you saw how he read the chart—he got every one of those animals wrong. And you told me he knows what all of them look like."

"Yes, sir, all his life he's known."

The doctor weighed his words for a moment, but 'Retha was sitting erect, waiting for him to tell her. "'Retha, I'm sorry. I think Ray is going blind."

'Retha stared at him. She'd managed somehow to get the money to pay for the first appointment. This couldn't be all he could tell her! "Well, what can you do?"

The doctor cleared his throat. What he was about to say wasn't easy. "There's nothing more that I can do. The ointment obviously didn't work. I can't stop his eyes from getting weaker and weaker."

Mama stared up at the doctor, her own eyes enormous. "My boy's going blind?"

The doctor hated to say it, but he thought he should tell her the truth. 'Retha was young—in her early twenties—but very strong inside. She would find a way to cope with things. Carefully he said to her, "You'll have to start thinking about how he's going to get around."

He was right; 'Retha was already thinking ahead. "Well, who can I talk to? Who knows how to help him?"

The doctor sighed. "I'm not sure. But I'll ask

around. And you can start asking around too. Someone in this town might have some ideas about where Ray can learn how to live his life without being able to see." He hesitated. "Of course, maybe it'll be easier for him than we think. People feel sorry for blind people."

'Retha stood up. Her back was very straight, and her eyes were snapping fire. "Nobody's going to feel sorry for my boy. I'm raising him to be a good, strong man, and even if he can't see, that's not gonna change. He's not gonna beg or depend on someone else. Even if he can't see, he's gonna walk tall. You'll see."

The doctor winced as she left to join Ray in the waiting room. In a poor town like Greenville, being blind would be a serious handicap for the boy. There were no other blind people in the whole town. To make matters worse for Ray, he was poor and black. The doctor just couldn't figure out how 'Retha was going to help Ray to "walk tall." He couldn't imagine what kind of life Ray would have now.

# Fighting the Shadows

Mama was determined that Ray would never be helpless, even if he did go blind. As they walked home from Dr. McCloud's office, she said to Ray, "Now, Ray, we're gonna show you how to get around. The doctor thinks you may not be able to see so good for a while."

Ray was full of questions he hadn't been able to ask the doctor. "How long, Mama? Will this goo on my eyes go away? Did he give you some more medicine for me?"

Mama spoke slowly. She needed time to think about what she wanted to say. At last, gently but firmly, she said, "Ray, there's times you just gotta face up to what happens to you in life. Sometimes it ain't real good. But the true test of a person is when the bad stuff happens and they get through it somehow. You know what I mean?"

Ray struggled to understand. "I think so, Mama. Like we got through when George died." He tried not to think about George, even now, a year after he'd died. Thinking of George still made him hurt too much.

Mama, though, was nodding. "That's right. Just like that. That was a hard time, and we had other hard times too, like when we had to move in with Mr. Pit and Miss Georgia for a while 'cause I couldn't get enough work. But we got through those, and we're gonna find a way to get through this."

"What's this bad time, Mama?"

Mama took a tighter grip on Ray's hand. She wouldn't let herself break down; she had to tell him bluntly but show him she had the strength to help him. "Well, this one's a pretty bad time too. Dr. McCloud's done his best for you, but it just ain't good enough. He thinks you're not goin' to see any better, Ray. He says he thinks it's gonna get worse. He says you're goin' blind."

Ray was silent for a minute. Blind! Not able to see anymore, ever?

He hadn't thought of anything to say when Mama spoke again. "There're things that happen to a person in life, Ray, and a strong person, well, he gets through and says, 'All right. I'll deal with it. I'll do what I have to do to get through this.' And then he does it, and comes out on the other side even stronger.

"The weak person—well, the weak person sits down and cries and tries to find someone to take care of him and decide things for him, 'cause he don't think he can do it himself. I don't ever want you to be a weak person, Ray. When you're strong, you can lick the world, if you have to. If you're weak, you're sunk. You understand me?"

Ray knew now was not the time to burst into tears. "Yes, Mama." But he couldn't resist a rush of questions. "How can I walk around if I can't see, Mama? How can I find my way?"

Mama tossed her head. "Well, if that ain't silly! You know this place like the back of your hand, don't you? Didn't you spend all your life here? Don't you know where everything is?"

"Well, yes'm, but—"

"No buts. Your legs ain't goin' blind. You can still walk, you can still run. You just gotta figure out a way to know what's around you so you don't get hurt. Most people use their eyes for that. I'll help you use other parts."

At home, Mary Jane listened silently as Mama told her in an unnaturally brisk voice what Dr. McCloud had said. Ray was feeling his way around the table, squinting at the dishes, using his fingers instead of his eyes to tell him if they were the right size for supper. He set the forks and knives out next to them.

Mary Jane motioned to Mama to step out of the kitchen so they could talk privately, without Ray's hearing. "'Retha, you gotta get him help," she said quietly. "One of them white canes so he can walk around and know what's in front of him. Or maybe one of them dogs that lead blind people around."

Mama listened to Mary Jane. She almost never got angry at Mary Jane, but this time her eyes were like ice. "My son," she said coldly, "will never carry a white cane, you hear me? Or use a dog to help him find his way around. Never! He's gonna walk proud, I tell you, walk proud *on his own*. I won't let him be some kind of cripple people have to feel sorry for. I'll teach him. I'll show him how to do it."

"But you don't know how, yourself," Mary Jane pleaded. "He's the only blind person in this town, 'Retha. How you gonna help him keep up with the other kids? He's got to have a cane, at least, so he don't walk into walls."

Ray was moving around the table, using the edges of the table to help him figure out where he was. He set down a glass at each place, saving his favorite blue glass, which he knew by its shape, for his own place.

Mama glanced at him, and her face, which had been hard, softened. "I tell you I won't let him be different from the other kids," she said quietly. "I'll never let him carry a white cane. Kids pick up on things like that real quick. If he starts off thinking he's not good enough for 'em, or can't keep up with 'em, he'll never fit in again. He'll always be different."

"But he is different," Mary Jane insisted. "He's bright, sure, but how you gonna send him to school to learn when he can't see the board, can't read the letters with his eyes?"

"We won't bother about school now," Mama retorted. "He's too young now. I can teach him what he needs to know, right here at home."

Mama was as good as her word. The next day, after she finished her laundry, she began to work with Ray, showing him how to use his ears and other senses to make up for his poor eyesight.

It was one of Ray's worst days so far. Everything around him was a blur. He could distinguish little but shadows. He listened hard for the sound of Mama's voice so he could tell where she was.

"Come on, Ray," she said, holding his arm. "Let's walk up to the front door. Now count with me." She took steps the same size as Ray's smaller stride. "One, two, three, four, five, six, seven." She stopped in front of the door, took his hand, and placed it on the door. "There? You feel that? That's right at the front door. Now how many steps did you take?"

"Seven, Mama."

"That's right. You remember that. Seven steps to the front door. You take eight and you'll walk into it. All right?"

"Yes, Mama. Seven steps."

They practiced going back and forth, with

Ray counting off the steps each time. Then Mama stepped back. "All right, Ray. You can do it by yourself. You show me now."

Ray straightened up. He knew it was seven steps to the front door. Proudly he counted off seven steps. Then he fell over a bush.

Mama didn't laugh at him. She helped him stand up and brushed off his shirt and pants. "Now, Ray, you just learned a good lesson. It's seven steps to the front door, but you went off in the wrong direction. You gotta go in the right direction or that countin' won't mean anything. Okay?"

Ray flushed. "Let me try again, Mama. I can do it better this time."

"All right, son. I'm watching."

Ray thought about what direction he was headed in. When he and Mama had practiced walking toward the house, the sun had been shining in his face. He remembered how good it felt across his cheek. Carefully he turned until he felt the same warm feeling on his face. There. That was the right way.

He counted off the steps again. "One, two, three, four, five, six, seven." He lifted his hand and reached in front of him. He was standing right at the front door.

He could hear the smile in Mama's voice. "That's good, Ray! That's very good!"

Next she showed Ray how to fold an arm across his chest so he wouldn't walk into things and hurt himself. The arm would keep him from getting hurt. His other arm would reach out, moving gently to and fro, so he didn't walk into things.

They practiced walking in the house, with Ray counting off steps from one wall to the other. In just a few minutes, he knew how many steps led to the bedroom or the kitchen. He knew where the small closet in the hall was.

By the time Ray lay down to sleep that night, he knew how to get around the whole house, the front yard, and the road in front of the house. He thought he heard Mama say to Mary Jane, "There, you see? He don't need no white cane."

But he was so tired, he couldn't be sure. His head was full of numbers, numbers that told him how many steps to take from one point to another. As he tried to remember them all, he dropped off to sleep.

# Saying Good-bye

"Ray, you done with that chopping yet?" Mama called. "It's almost time for supper."

"Almost done, Mama," Ray called back from the yard. It was summer again, and the air was warm on his arms. It was too hot to chop wood, but Mama had told him to do it, and he knew she meant what she said. Besides, he was pretty big now—almost seven—and boys that big had to work.

He felt with his foot for the long block of wood in front of him. Good. It was right where he expected it to be, right where he'd set it.

Carefully he raised the ax above his head and, a moment later, brought it crashing down. He heard the *crunch* of the wood splitting apart. He smiled. He'd chopped that whole basket of wood into pieces just the right size for the stove. Mama would sure be pleased.

Behind him, one of the neighbor women gasped. "'Retha, what are you doin'? You crazy?"

He heard her rushing toward the screen door, yanking it open, and letting it slam behind her. He also heard what she said to Mama.

"'Retha, what are you doin', makin' that boy chop wood? He'll chop off his own foot one of these days! What are you thinkin' of, lettin' him use that ax and he can't even see his own hand in front of his face?"

Mama's voice came back at him, firm as always. "He's blind, but he ain't stupid. I showed him how to do it, and he does it. Better for him to make his own way than think folks are gonna make life easy for him just 'cause he's blind."

Ray carefully set the ax against the side of the house, where it belonged, and gathered up the wood he'd chopped into the basket, which he carried into the house. As Mama had taught him, he carried the basket in one hand and held the other in front of him, using it to check for obstacles so he didn't bump into anything. He got up the porch and inside the house just fine, as he'd done for a year now, since he began to go blind.

Inside the house, Ray deposited the wood carefully next to the stove and said, "Hello, Miz Mary," politely to his neighbor, acting as though he hadn't heard what she'd said about him.

"Hello, Ray," his neighbor replied. "How're the eyes these days?"

"Oh, fine," Ray said. It was true that his eyes didn't hurt. But by now, all he could make out, even when he tried his hardest, were a few shadows. He couldn't even recognize his mother's face anymore, though he always knew her by her quick, light footsteps, her smell, and her voice.

The neighbor hesitated. "Guess you stay pretty busy," she said finally.

"Yes'm. I help Mama with the chores. There's a lot to do 'round here. I'm the man of the house, you know."

"You're a good man, Ray," the neighbor told him. She put her hand for a moment on his dark head. "Maybe you're right, 'Retha. Maybe I'm wrong."

Ray heard the door squeak on its hinges as she pushed it open and the soft thud as she let it drop behind her. As she went down the porch steps, he thought he also heard her give a choked sob.

"Supper, Ray," Mama said. He could smell the good hot smell of turnip greens and pork. He got down the plates from the cupboard and felt his way around the table, putting one at each place, one for him, one for Mama, and one for Mary Jane, who still ate supper with them every night when she got back from her job at the mill. Ray felt very lucky having two women who acted like his mother, and he loved and obeyed both of them.

When he'd set out the plates, he got out their forks and knives, setting them neatly at each place. He'd done that for a long time now. Mama had shown him how to do lots of things since he first started going blind, from walking in the road, to putting on his clothes the right way and buttoning them up properly. She treated him as though he could still see. She encouraged him to play and run races with his friends, all of whom could see. Ray would run as fast as he could, after checking before the race to see that the way was clear and there were no potholes or obstructions in the road. As he ran, he could hear the other boys around him and knew when to speed up to get ahead of them.

Though his sight was almost gone now, he relied on his other senses to help him experience the world. His senses of hearing, smell, and taste were sharper than ever. He could get around just fine, and true to her word, Mama had refused to get him a white cane. She said using a white cane marked you as different, and she didn't want anyone thinking Ray was different.

They still had to wipe the gooey film out of his eyes every morning, but Ray didn't feel any different from any of his friends. They still played together; they still shouted and ran and had ball games. And he was right there in the thick of it with all of them.

One other thing remained the same too. Ray still loved playing music with his friend Mr. Pit. Though he could no longer see the keys of the piano, his little fingers could unerringly find the keys he wanted to play. Mr. Pit helped by placing Ray's hands on the keys when Ray first started playing, so Ray would know where the middle of the keyboard was. With every passing day, Ray's love of music grew stronger, and he wanted to learn about it.

Tonight, Mama and Mary Jane were quieter than usual. They said little beyond asking Ray if he wanted more pork or more milk. Ray could feel that something was in the air, but he couldn't guess what it was.

Afterward, as he curled into a comfortable blanket on the floor, where it was cooler, the soft murmur of voices came to him. Mama and Mary Jane thought they were talking too quietly for him to hear, but Ray's hearing was practically as good as that of the heroes in comic books.

"'Retha, you don't pay no attention to that woman," Mary Jane said. "She just likes to stir up trouble."

Ray could hear Mama sigh. "Maybe, but every so often even a frog makes sense when it croaks. Truth is, Mary Jane, I can't teach Ray no more here. I got to get him in front of people who can teach him. He stays with me, he won't learn how to do nuthin'—and then what kind of life will he have? Poor and black

62

and blind—how's he gonna make his way in this world?"

"But where can he go?"

"I don't know. But I'll find out. There's got to be somebody who can teach a blind boy. Ray's smart. He can learn. But he'll never learn nuthin' here if there ain't no one to help him."

There was some rustling of the bedsheets, then silence. Ray lay in bed and wondered: Who could teach him the things Mama thought he had to learn?

Mama didn't take long to find out. She put on her cleanest cotton dress and the hat she wore to church on Sundays. She asked everyone she knew how to find a school for blind children. When her neighbors and other black people in town had no answers, she ventured on, asking white people she knew if they had any ideas. She was polite but persistent. She just had to find out what she could do for Ray.

Finally, she learned of a state school in St. Augustine.

St. Augustine was in Florida, but hundreds of miles from Greenville. The school taught both blind and deaf children. Not only did the students learn subjects like reading and arithmetic, the school also taught them skills they could use to get jobs, so they could earn a living. The blind children also learned Braille, a system of reading raised dots with the tips of their fingers. This helped them read books and magazines for the blind. Using Braille could help them stay in touch with the rest of the world.

St. Augustine was a good solution. Ray could live there and learn for most of the year. Then, during the summers, he could come home and live with Mama and Mary Jane. It meant that from now on, Ray would be away from his only family for almost all of the year. But it was the only way Mama could find that he could get an education.

There was no money to send Ray to this school. But Mama managed to get him accepted as a charity student, which meant someone else who wanted to help a blind child paid his way. Though Mama had always refused to accept charity in any form, this time she agreed: She knew that St. Augustine could help Ray lead a normal life.

Mama explained to Ray that he would be leaving home and traveling to St. Augustine on the train. There would be lots of St. Augustine students on the same train, but Mama couldn't afford a train ticket for herself. She had just enough to pay for Ray's ticket. Ray would travel to St. Augustine by himself.

Ray burst into tears when he heard this. "No, Mama, don't make me go away!" he pleaded. "I'm the man of the house! I do chores for you! Please don't make me go, Mama! I want to stay here with you and Mary Jane and Mr. Pit. I got plenty to do here. I don't need to go anywhere!"

But Mama insisted. Sitting on the edge of the bed, with her hand in his soft hair, she said, "Ray, we got to get you an education. Can't get one here. There's no school around that can take a boy who can't see. This school can teach you what you need to know, things I can't teach you. We're all gonna miss you here, Ray. But you got to go."

Ray cried and cried. He thought his heart was going to break. Leaving home by himself—going off to someplace he'd never been before—away from everyone he'd ever known and loved . . . this couldn't be happening!

But it was. Mama took him into town and managed to pay for him to have a suit of new clothes, finer than he'd ever worn before. The pants and jacket were made from the same soft material, and there were two nice shirts that went with it. The clothes had all been worn by someone else before, but Ray didn't know it. He had never owned a nice suit before. Even going to church, he just wore his nicest, cleanest pants and a clean shirt.

Mama and Ray packed his clothes into a cheap, cardboard suitcase. It wasn't very big or very sturdy, but Ray didn't have very much to put in it. All the while he packed, the tears were running down his cheeks. But he knew Mama. Once she decided something, that was that. She wasn't going to change her mind.

Finally the day in September came when Ray had to leave Greenville on the train. Mama took him to the station. He could hear the shouts and laughter of other children on the train as they climbed on the train and greeted their friends: "Hey, you going back again?" "Yeah, time to get back to school." "You have a good summer?" "Sure did; caught about a million catfish. How 'bout you?" "I caught two million!"

Ray didn't have anyone to talk to. The sounds of the other children's laughter made him feel even worse. He was all alone.

Mama let him stand with her on the train

platform until just before the train left. She knew how bad he felt. Quietly she said to him, "Now, Ray, this may seem real bad to you now, but just remember, you're gonna learn a lot of new things you couldn't learn here. You're gonna read and write and all kinds of things. These people at St. Augustine got all kinds of knowledge; you pay attention to 'em. This school is gonna be real good for you."

"Yes, Mama," Ray said tonelessly. He turned away from her and blinked hard, trying to keep the tears from coursing down his cheeks again.

He heard a sharp whistle and what sounded like a soft puff. "Train's about ready to leave," Mama said. Her small hand gripped his very tightly. "We got to put you on it in a minute.

"Now just remember, Ray," Mama went on, "there's always another way in life to do what you want to do. If you can't do things one way, find another way. Will you remember that?"

"Yes, Mama," Ray said. The tears were pouring freely down his face now, and he didn't care who saw it. "I'll remember. Find another way."

"That's right." She kissed him and hugged him very tightly, just once. "Come on, let's get you on the train."

By the time she got him settled in his seat, Ray felt worse than ever. This strange, pulsing engine beneath him was going to move off in a moment, taking him away from Mama and Mary Jane for months and months. He didn't think he could stand it.

"Remember," Mama whispered to him just before she left the train, "you can always find another way."

Ray didn't know he'd just been given the best advice he'd ever get. He was too busy weeping to know that Mama was still standing on the train platform and that as the train pulled out, she was weeping too.

# Valuable Lessons

"Hey, Foots! We're havin' a race. You wanna come?"

It was one of the boys in his class at St. Augustine. Ray looked up listlessly when he heard the voice.

He'd been at school for a few weeks now, and he still cried himself to sleep every night. He missed Mama and Mary Jane so much! It hurt every time he thought of them—and he couldn't stop thinking of them.

It didn't help that school was so different from anything he'd ever known before. Ray had arrived with his few clothes in a cheap suitcase. Everyone else had stiff new shoes. Ray had none. He'd never owned a pair of shoes in his life.

Since he was a charity student, he was given a pair of shoes to wear. They felt strange on his feet, enclosing his toes when he was used to squishing them through the dust and mud of the streets back home. Here, he had to wear shoes every day.

When the other boys learned he didn't have any shoes to wear, they started calling him "Foots." They had all settled in quickly to their rooms and their studies. Ray was still miserable. It gave them another reason to taunt him.

Now, though, the boy's voice sounded friendly as he said, "We'll race holding on to a wire so we'll know we're going in the right direction. Other end's held by a kid at the finish line. You wanna come?"

Ray thought. It might have been the first

time anyone had asked him to join them at play. Usually he spent recesses by himself, moping around the school yard.

"Okay," he said, getting up from his bed. "Sounds like fun."

They got out to the yard where they played during recess. The boy put Ray's hand on the wire. "You just follow that to the finish line," he said. "Run as fast as you can." He hesitated for a moment. "'Course, if you was to run without holdin' the wire, you'd prob'ly beat us all. But I guess you can't do that."

Ray had done a lot of running without any help back home. A spark of pride rose in his chest. "I guess I can. You just follow the wire. I'll be waitin' at the finish line."

Before he ran, though, he carefully removed his shoes and put them in a corner away from the race area. He knew he'd run faster barefoot.

Ray could hear a dozen boys lining up to run. One of the boys turned him. "You go that way," he said, holding Ray's arm out in front of him. Ray nodded. He understood which way he had to run.

Someone yelled, "Ready, set, *go!*" Ray took off, running as fast as he could in the direction they'd faced him in. He could feel himself running faster than everyone else, could hear the others dropping back behind him.

It felt so *good* to run this fast again! He was going to beat these boys inside out. He was going to beat them faster than they'd ever been beat. He was going to—

Bang!

Ray's head slammed into a heavy iron post. They hadn't told him it was there. He reeled away from the post and fell to his knees on the ground. Behind him, he could hear several of the boys laughing.

They'd deliberately tricked him. They'd let him run faster than everyone else, knowing he'd slam into the iron post. Tears poured down his face, not just from the pain in his

head but also from the betrayal. No one had ever done anything like that to him in his life. Never. But here at St. Augustine, it seemed something like this happened every day.

"Hey, Foots, you won!" one of the boys shouted behind him. "Don't you want to pick up your trophy?"

"That crybaby?" someone else jeered. "All he ever does, every day, is cry his eyes out for his mama. Cries so loud, I can't hear myself think. Maybe he should go back home to her so he can stop crying and we can have some peace around here."

Ray walked slowly away, rubbing his bruised head until he couldn't hear the laughter and jeers anymore. He knew where he was by the fresh air around him. He also knew there were no obstacles on the field; the school had made certain of it.

His teachers had brought him out here when he first arrived and shown him the field, walking him from one end to the other so he got an idea of the size of it. Unlike the other boys, many of whom had been blind from birth, Ray didn't use the traditional white cane that blind people carried to help them negotiate when they were walking around. Because Mama had always pushed him to walk and run at home as he always had, he had little fear of falling or dealing with obstacles.

Ray got to the door of his dormitory and started to open it. "No, Ray!" called the voice of one of his teachers. "You're in the wrong place!"

Ray stopped. He heard the teacher, a young man, come up next to him. "This is the dormitory for the white boys," the teacher explained. "You don't want to go in there. Your dormitory is in the next row. Here, I'll show you."

The teacher walked Ray to the correct door and put his hand on the knob. "You want me to go up with you?"

"No, sir. I can find it okay," Ray said. He was puzzled. He knew back in Greenville white folks and black folks lived in different parts of town, to separate them. White folks there didn't want to see black people in their part of town.

But here, everybody was *blind*. Some were deaf. If you couldn't even see what color somebody was or hear the sound of his voice, did you still have to be separated? Did it still matter so much?

He didn't realize he'd spoken his thoughts out loud, until the teacher answered firmly, "Yes, Ray, it does matter. So you stay in your dorm with the black students and you let the white students alone in their dorm. You understand now?"

"Yes, sir," Ray said numbly.

He made his way up to his room easily, but his heart was sore and bewildered. He just didn't see why this white-and-black business was so important to grown-ups. People were people, weren't they? Wasn't that all that mattered?

One thing was sure, though. The race today had taught him a valuable lesson, and Ray was quick to catch on to lessons of all kinds. The boys had laughed at him because he'd cried. They'd let him run into a post to make him cry. He was finished crying. He'd still miss Mama and Mary Jane, but it was time to get down to learning, which was why Mama had sent him here in the first place. He'd see them at Christmas, even if that seemed awfully far away right now.

But Ray wasn't about to let those boys make him feel bad anymore. It was time to show the people at St. Augustine what he could do. It was time to stop crying. There was something good here, and he was going to find it.

# Learning Another Way

"Ray, that's good!" praised his teacher. "You read that whole page of Braille perfectly!"

Ray smiled. He'd just turned seven a few weeks after starting at St. Augustine, and he'd finally gotten interested in his schoolwork. There was nothing to this Braille business. Mama would be so pleased when he told her in his letters home that he could now read Braille.

Braille is a system of raised dots that blind people read with their fingertips. Each arrangement of dots stands for a certain letter of the alphabet. If you put the dots together, you can spell out a word. Put enough dots together and you can spell out sentences, and then paragraphs. When you pass your fingers over them and feel how the dots arranged on the page, you know what the dots stand for. It is the same as a person with sight looking at a word made of individual letters on a printed page and knowing right away what it means.

"I can't believe how fast you learned it!" his teacher went on. "It's only been ten days since you really buckled down to this. You're one of the fastest Braille readers at school."

Ray glowed. He was proud of how fast he had mastered Braille. Now he could read at lightning speed, his fingers passing swiftly over the arrangements of dots on a page of Braille. He wrote letters home to Mama regularly now, telling her what he was doing and learning. A teacher took down his words with a pen and paper and put Mama's address on the envelope. Ray knew Mama loved getting his letters. He also knew that every time he could report he was doing well, she was proud of him.

When she wrote back, the same teacher took out her letter and read it out loud to Ray. Ray would memorize the short sentences Mama wrote and hug them close to his heart, so he could remember them when he was lying in bed at night. It made him feel like Mama was closer to him.

Ray was making progress in other areas too. He had always liked doing things with his hands, even years ago when he and George played together at home. Now he was using those same hands to learn new crafts.

The blind boys were taught to make chair seats out of cane so they could get jobs when they were finished with school. Being blind, there were many jobs they wouldn't be able to do. Learning to make chair seats was a skill that didn't require vision. It was the school's way of preparing them for the future.

Ray's shop teacher noticed his sure hands. He made wonderful cane-bottom chairs out of dried reeds woven tightly together. It was a special skill, and Ray caught on right away. His nimble fingers learned to weave the reeds together tightly, more tightly than any of the other boys, so they remained strong and wouldn't come apart. The chairs he made would last for years.

Best of all, though, St. Augustine had real music classes. The students were taught to play instruments, along with music theory.

Thanks to Mr. Pit, Ray was way ahead of the other students who were just starting to learn to play the piano. Now, though, he was given a glimpse into a more complex part of the music world.

"All right, Ray," his music teacher said a few weeks later. "Play me that combination again. Eighth note, eighth note, and then two sixteenth notes. Here, I'll play it first."

Ray listened as the teacher played the combination. Those were two eighth notes. They were played longer than the sixteenth notes, which were played very fast. The quarter notes were held longer than the eighth notes, and half notes, of course, were held twice as long. Whole notes were held for a whole measure of music.

Ray caught on to the idea right away. Mr. Pit hadn't taught him any music theory when they played together; they just played things they liked and listened to good music on the jukebox. Now Ray was learning that you could write down notes on special paper that had five horizontal lines and five spaces between them, called a musical staff, and other people could then play it just the way you wrote it. Of course, he couldn't write it down—there was no Braille notation for musical notes— but he could learn why he was playing certain notes and combinations and how to put them together correctly.

Here at St. Augustine, Miss Mallard, the

music teacher, taught students as many instruments as they'd like to learn. Students who were interested in learning more were encouraged to come to harder classes. Ray was one of those who couldn't get enough. When he heard his idol, Artie Shaw, playing the clarinet on the radio with his own big band, Ray wanted to learn to play clarinet too.

Miss Mallard, seeing his interest, had agreed to teach him. He didn't know what to make of the odd-sounding instrument at first, but quickly began to catch on. He understood that the notes he played on the clarinet were the same ones Mr. Pit had taught him on the piano long ago.

Music theory was a little harder. That meant how different notes and chords were written down on a musical staff to produce certain sounds. Sometimes it was confusing, but Ray loved it.

Now, Ray played the new combination of

notes three times on the piano, just as he'd been asked: eighth note, eighth note, and two sixteenth notes. "That's it," Miss Mallard told him. "Now let's go on to the next measures. Two half notes, then a whole note and an eighth and two sixteenths."

Ray didn't even need to run his fingers over the music again. He had memorized it already. His fingers touched the right keys unerringly, his heart soaring at the sounds coming from the piano. It was almost like the days when he used to play with Mr. Pit.

When he finished, Miss Mallard patted his shoulder. "Great work, Ray. Now you practice that combination on the clarinet tonight. I'll hear it tomorrow."

"Can I play it for you on the piano, too?" Ray asked eagerly.

She laughed. "Yes, on the piano, too! You sure do love to play that piano, don't you?"

Ray heard another sound at the door of the music room, a special whistle. One of his friends had come in. The lesson must have run a lot longer than he thought. Ray noticed that Miss Mallard always gave him a few extra minutes, maybe more than the others, because she saw that he loved it so.

Ray cocked his head at the door. "What's up, Sam?"

"Come on, Foots, we're all waiting!" said Sam, exasperated. By now, "Foots" was an affectionate nickname. Once Ray stopped being homesick, the boys discovered he was lots of fun. Ray could run faster and farther than any boy in his class, and the others knew it. Still, they loved running races against him, hoping every time they would win. But they just didn't understand his fascination with all this music theory junk. "Aren't you finished with that music stuff yet?"

"In a little while," Ray answered absently. He did love to run races, and he loved to win. But the more he learned at St. Augustine about music, the more exciting it became to him. Every single day there was something new to learn. The younger students learned how to play various instruments. Older students learned music theory, composition, and even how to arrange songs using various instruments. Ray couldn't wait to learn those things. The teachers told him real musicians made up their own arrangements of songs. He wanted to try it!

St. Augustine was an ideal atmosphere for Ray. He took all the regular subjects every school taught, and found that he liked math almost as much as music. Since music is based on mathematical principles, it made sense that Ray always enjoyed it. And the special music classes Ray took every day only increased his hunger to learn more. He couldn't soak it up fast enough.

Since St. Augustine was primarily a school to teach blind and deaf children, teachers focused on helping students adjust to their disabilities. They learned to sense obstacles in their paths, so they could move around them safely. They learned to fine-tune their other senses, to help them compensate for being blind or deaf.

Ray learned to use his keen hearing to know when he was passing a doorway or a break in a wall that wasn't solid—a little rush of air from the doorway would let him know. He wore hard-soled shoes, so he could hear his own footsteps, which helped him know whether the place he was in was large or small. By now he had gotten used to the hard leather enclosing his toes. He learned to listen for others' footsteps as well. That way, he knew if someone was coming toward him or away from him and where they were in relation to him. It helped him get around without bumping into anyone.

Unlike other students at St. Augustine, Ray never used a white cane, as many blind people did. Because Mama had taught him to get around without one when he first went blind, he was sure-footed and used his hands with confidence. Because she wanted him to be independent, Ray too wanted to be independent. He needed less coddling from his teachers than other students, and he memorized directions faster. He wasn't afraid of bumping into something, but the teachers noticed and marveled that he seldom bumped into anything even though he moved faster than almost any student at school. He wore thick glasses to protect his eyes from picking up dust in the air, but they did nothing to help the dark shadows he could still see become any clearer.

Ray wasn't thinking about that. He just knew that while he still missed Mama and Mary Jane, St. Augustine was teaching him all kinds of new things. He was making friends. Other students noticed his confidence and curiosity. What his teachers noticed was that no matter how well Ray did in his reading and arithmetic classes or how much interest he showed in making those cane-bottom chairs, nothing excited him as much as music.

# The Final Darkness

There was no way around it: It hurt when Christmas vacation came and Ray couldn't go home to visit Mama and Mary Jane. Mama had written that she wanted him home, but Ray knew there was no money to pay for his train fare. There was no other way for him to get home.

So he spent Christmas in the big school building, alone except for a few teachers who were also staying. The sounds of his class-mates' chatter and laughter were far away as he imagined them with their families, opening presents, having fun. Ray felt very sorry for himself. Being blind was no big deal. Being poor and black wasn't so hard. But being away from his family at Christmas was awful. Worst of all, he felt like the only person who'd ever been away from his family at Christmas. He hated it.

He moped around through the whole vacation, but brightened when everyone else came back. Now life would start again. Now he could go back to his regular lessons and learn more about the subject he couldn't seem to get enough of: music.

But a few weeks later, Ray's right eye began to burn. A lot of the time, it burned so badly that he wanted to cover his face to stop the pain. But nothing stopped the pain. Instead it got more and more painful, every day.

Finally, one day in his music class, he had to stop playing. This was so unusual for Ray that Miss Mallard immediately asked him what was wrong.

"My eye," Ray whispered. He took off his glasses and dug his fist into his eye, trying to stop the pain. "It hurts so much."

"Turn your face up to me. I'll take a look at it." Obediently Ray turned his face upward. He felt the teacher moving her finger lightly over his cheek.

There was a silence. Then Miss Mallard said, "All right, Ray. You're going to the infirmary. We'll let the nurse look at you."

The nurse saw that the eye was red and inflamed. Ray was now crying with the pain of it. She bathed the eye in a soothing solution, but the pain did not stop. "He needs to see a doctor," she said to Ray's music teacher.

The doctor who visited St. Augustine regularly was called in to look at Ray's eye. He examined it grimly. The eye, behind Ray's protective glasses, was bulging.

"Well, Ray, I'll have to talk to some other doctors about this," the doctor said. He wrote something on his prescription pad, tore off the top sheet, and gave it to the nurse. "This will help dull the pain so you can get some sleep," he told Ray.

Ray spent several nights in the infirmary instead of his own bed. The pain in his eye constantly bothered him. He couldn't seem to think of anything else, though he concentrated hard on Mama, Mary Jane, his music, anything he could think of. It was no use. The pain overrode everything.

One morning, after Ray had finally fallen asleep, exhausted, after midnight, the doctor came in, bringing a few other people with them. Ray could hear several sets of footsteps and the soft murmur of voices. Finally, he heard the footsteps move toward him. "Ray, this is Dr. Brown," said the doctor.

Ray nodded. He knew the voice.

"Ray, I'm sorry, that eye is infected. We can't do anything to stop it, and we've got to get that pain to stop. I'm afraid we're going to have to remove your eye altogether."

Ray's mouth went dry. "You're gonna—you're gonna take out my eye?"

"I'm sorry, Ray. But I promise when it's over, you won't hurt anymore."

Ray went to the local hospital the next day. The following day, the doctor operated on his eye.

It wasn't as bad as Ray had thought. Everyone at the hospital, even the white doctors and nurses, were kind to him. They brought him special foods and made sure they spent time just talking with him. When they found out how much he loved music, they coaxed him to sing for them.

Ray stayed in the hospital for a few days. A week later, he was back in classes at St. Augustine. A month later, he'd almost forgotten the operation.

The only difference was that now, there were no more shadows. Now there was just darkness, every hour of every day. But Ray was sturdy and optimistic. Being blind couldn't stop him from playing his music, or doing anything he wanted to do. Thanks to Mama and the people at St. Augustine, he could keep on going. In spite of the darkness, Ray hadn't lost anything that really mattered.

# The Lazy Days of Summer

In May, Ray took the train home to Greenville. But this time, he was full of confidence. He had learned Braille, he had lived away from Mama for eight months, and he knew so much more about music!

There wasn't much he *couldn't* do, he thought. He was so proud of showing Mama and Mary Jane how he could read with his fingers and play the clarinet. He was so happy showing Mr. Pit how much more he knew about playing the piano now.

What was even better was showing his old friends, who had stayed here in Greenville, just how much he could do. He could run as fast and jump as high as all of them, and with all he knew of his hometown, he didn't need anyone's help to get around.

"Lookit that!"

Ray's friends looked admiringly at the two-wheeled bicycle leaning up against his house. "Hey, Ray, is that yours?"

"Sure it's mine," Ray said, trying to sound casual, as though he got a new bike every day. "Looks pretty good, doesn't it?" He ran his hand happily over the smooth chrome.

"Good? It's fantastic!" The boys all knelt by him, looking at the tires, trying out the horn strapped to the handlebars. It made a loud, ugly sound. Ray winced. The other boys laughed.

"Where'd you get it?" asked one skeptical boy.

Ray shrugged. "It was waiting for me when I got home. I guess Mama and Mary Jane got it for me." He was trying to sound as cool as possible, though he was bursting with pride. Few of the other boys had ever

ridden a bicycle, let alone owned one.

He wasn't going to tell them that when he got off the train and heard Mama's voice and felt her arms around him, he had dissolved in happy tears. It was so good to be back home, after all these months! With all the activity at St. Augustine, he hadn't realized how wonderful it would be to come back to Greenville for the summer.

Now he tried to act as though he knew all the answers to the boys' eager questions.

"It's blue," his friend Wilbur said tentatively. "Did you know it was blue?"

Ray nodded. "Mama told me. She told me it was almost the color of the sky."

"It sure is." The boys stopped then, and hesitated.

Ray wondered at the silence. "What's up?" he finally asked.

"How you gonna ride it?" his friend Johnny asked curiously. Ray always called him Johnny Cake. "I mean, do you have to tie it onto someone else's bike?"

"What for?" Ray asked, though he had a good idea what Johnny meant.

Johnny struggled to say what he meant without being rude. "Well, I mean—if you tie your bike to someone else's, they can lead the way, and . . ." His voice trailed off.

Ray scoffed. "Don't need no one to lead the way. Ain't this Greensville? Ain't I lived here practically my whole life? Don't I know every stone and tree in it? Come on!"

It took him just a few minutes to catch on to the idea of balance on the bike, but as soon as he did, Ray was determined to lead the others, not be left behind.

The other boys who owned bikes ran home, while Ray practiced riding up and down in front of his house. He listened carefully for the sounds of voices or even the unusual sound of a truck. Not too many people in the black side of Greenville owned a truck, and few trucks ever drove through there, but Ray knew he had to listen for them, anyway. Even after months at St. Augustine, remembering the curves and turns of the road in front of him was a snap.

When the boys came back, Ray listened till he heard them cluster around him. "Everybody ready?" he shouted. "Come on, let's go down to the swimming hole!"

And before anyone else could start, he was off, pedaling furiously down the street, as easily as if he could see every tree and stone in it.

How Ray loved riding that bike! The more he rode, the more confident he became. He never fell off, not once. He never hurt himself or rode near anything dangerous. He rode so fast that Mama's neighbors clucked to her, "Seems like that boy's vision is twenty-twenty, 'stead of nothin'-nothin'."

Mama just smiled as she watched Ray ride. Getting that bike hadn't been easy for her and Mary Jane. They'd saved for months and gone without things they needed so it would be here waiting when he came home. But oh, what it meant to Ray!

Mr. Pit was so proud of Ray. Ray had learned so much in a year that he'd already gone further than Mr. Pit, and he was eager for more and more. Next year, he told Mr. Pit during one of their playing times, they would start to teach him how to arrange music—how to decide which instruments in a band played which notes so the whole sounded great.

"RC, you sure are growin'," Mr. Pit would say, shaking his head as he listened to the sounds Ray's growing fingers were making. Even without being able to see, Ray knew just how to pound that keyboard.

Being back in Greenville made Ray aware of how much he'd learned in his first year at St. Augustine. His friends, who were used to thinking of him as blind, stopped thinking about it. Ray was always at the center of the fun during the summer.

Mama was still doing laundry for white people, and Mary Jane was still working at the sawmill.

They still served him big, delicious dinners filled with country vegetables and fresh, luscious fruit. And Mama still insisted that Ray always remember to be independent. Some of the boys at his school had dogs who helped them get around. Ray mentioned it at dinner one night, just to hear what Mama would say about it.

Mama, as he'd thought, was completely against the idea. "Dogs are for people who are helpless," she insisted. "You're not helpless, Ray. You can do things as good as anyone, and that's the way it's always going to be."

Ray just grinned when he heard that, and helped himself to more of Mama's good fried chicken. He liked being able to do things for himself as much as Mama did. He had no intention of letting others take care of him and fuss over him. Having people feel sorry for you wasn't the way to get along in this world.

Besides, Ray reflected, if he ever let people feel sorry for him, Mama would be sure to hear of it, and she'd never let him get away with it.

# Budding Musician

Life settled into a routine: Fall, winter, and spring at St. Augustine, going to classes, doing homework, working in shop class, and learning more and more about music. Summer was his time to be with Mama and Mary Jane in Greenville, spend time with his old friends, jam with Mr. Pit on that old piano that always sounded so fine.

Ray had joined the school choir by the age of nine, and he was the youngest member. His music teachers, Miss Mallard, Mrs. Lawrence, and Miss Ryan, were teaching him to play classical music. Ray had never heard of Chopin or Mozart before, but he was learning their music. It was a whole different kind of sound, but he loved it. The down-home boogie-woogie that Mr. Pit had taught him—the blues—were never played in school. The teachers said that serious musicians learned the classics. Boogie-woogie wasn't real music. Ray didn't care. It was the music he'd been raised on, and he loved it all his life.

He also loved the musical stars of the day. Artie Shaw, who had his own big band and played clarinet beautifully, was one of Ray's favorites. It was Shaw who had inspired Ray to learn the clarinet in the first place, but what that man could do with it! Listening to Shaw play "Stardust" or "Concerto for Clarinet" was almost enough to make Ray cry. No one could play clarinet like Shaw, though Ray tried, every single day. He was determined to learn everything he could about all facets of music.

Ray listened to the radio at school that played Glenn Miller and Tommy Dorsey and Glen Gray and Benny Goodman. As his teachers began to show him how to arrange music, he listened to these big bands even more carefully, trying to pick out the various parts written for reeds, horns, and drums. When he understood why they'd done certain things with their musical arrangements, he got a thrill inside.

Ray was also one of the few blind students at St. Augustine who ever tried to communicate with the deaf students, who were separated from the blind students so they could learn to cope with their own unique problems. In order to do this, he learned sign language, where the deaf students would spell words into his hand. In turn, he'd speak to them, and they would read his lips. He thought it was fun.

Like most confident boys, he eventually got into trouble for the usual reasons. He'd throw spitballs while the teacher was out of the classroom or do something else that was forbidden. If other students told the teachers about Ray's misbehavior, Ray would wait patiently to pay them back. One of his favorite methods was to tie a piece of wire between two posts and wait for the student to come down the hall. Ray always was very pleased when he heard the thud of the student falling on his face. He considered that after that, they were even.

So time went on, with Ray cramming more and more music into his life. And as he did, little by little, he was also growing up.

Fall, winter, spring, summer . . . fall, winter, spring, summer . . .

Time went by, and Ray's boyhood chubbiness fell away, and he began to shoot up. And with a longer body and more years under his belt, he began to long for more independence.

The teachers, seeing his budding musical

skill, invited him to play the piano at after-noon tea parties held by some of the black ladies in town. Because the parties were meant to be elegant, Ray played only those songs he thought the ladies would feel comfortable hearing, popular songs like "String of Pearls" and "Jersey Bounce."

The ladies applauded politely when Ray finished and invited him to help himself to some of their candy or fruit. Ray especially loved getting tangerines, which were his favorite. Sometimes the ladies would collect a handful of coins for him. Often it amounted to two or three dollars, and when it did, Ray thought he was rich.

As Ray grew older, he found that one of the greatest joys of coming home from St. Augustine for the summer was the opportu-nity to earn a little money on his own, playing music. When he was around eleven, word of his playing ability began to circulate around Greenville. The result was that he was asked to play piano in some local clubs. He would play for an entire evening, sometimes five or six hours, and be paid a few dollars.

He was always the youngest musician on the bandstand, usually by at least ten years. Spending all those hours in the company of young men instead of boys his own age, Ray began to grow up very quickly. He began to think more as a professional, because when he was playing the piano in a club, no one would excuse him for making a mistake or not paying attention to the band's cues. If he was there to play and be paid like the others, he was supposed to act as mature as the others, be responsible, give his best.

It was good training for a boy who wanted to sing and play music for a living.

By this time, Ray knew that this was what he wanted to do with his life. The teachers at St. Augustine were training him to make cane-bottomed chairs, to act like a blind person and accept a blind person's limitations for his life. Ray didn't accept any limitations. The boy who sped down the streets of Greenville on a bike faster than his seeing friends thought if he could play as well as other musicians, he could get jobs being a musician. It was all he wanted.

Ray spent more and more time playing in clubs around Greenville during his summer vacations. Sometimes he'd get jobs as far away as Tallahassee, so the other members of the band would have to pick him up in their car. He loved the excitement, the music, and the sounds of people enjoying themselves. He loved learning what different bands needed and trying to fit in with different groups.

But he couldn't help noticing that when there were white musicians, the club owners treated them with more respect. He heard they were also paid considerably more than the black musicians. And since Ray had been listening to and studying musicians all his life, he was rapidly developing a good sense of who was and who was not a good musician. He thought musicians should be paid according to their ability, not their skin color.

He also noticed that the black musicians he played with, no matter how old they were, were always quiet and respectful to the club owners. But as he came off the bandstand night after night, he could feel the rage and frustration coming from them. If they'd tried to get into these clubs as patrons, they'd have been turned away. They were allowed in only because they were musicians. They shouldn't expect to get the same pay, when they were lucky even to be allowed inside.

That was the way it was, the other black musicians told him. No use trying to change it. This was Florida, and black musicians would never make as much money as white musicians. "Get used to it, boy," advised one of his bandmates, a guitarist, after a long night's playing in a Greenville club. "You play piano for a living, that's the way your life's gonna be too."

Ray listened, all right. But deep down inside, he didn't believe it would always have to be that way.

# Going It Alone

Ray was listening to a lecture in his math class when he heard the door open quietly. For a moment, he didn't pay any attention: He was busy thinking about the problem his math teacher had given them and he was working it out in his head.

Then another teacher was tapping him on the shoulder. "Ray? You're to come with me. Right now."

It was early May, and he would soon be heading home for another summer in Greenville. He was fifteen, and by now he knew that he could make all the extra money he wanted playing piano in the local bars.

It was a wonderful thought.

"What is it?" he said.

"You have to see the principal."

"Now?" Ray asked. He racked his brain for a minute. What had he done that they were pulling him out of class to punish him for? They never did that. And he couldn't think of any mischief he'd been into recently.

The teacher refused to answer any more questions. "You have to see the principal," was all she would say, hurrying Ray along the corridors.

But in the principal's office, there was a heavy, ominous silence. "Sit down, Ray," said the principal, and the teacher showed Ray to a soft chair near his desk.

Ray sat, but his thoughts were buzzing like gnats around a watermelon patch. What was going on?

"Ray," the principal said softly. "Ray—I just

don't know how to say this to you." To Ray, the principal didn't sound angry. He sounded uncertain, even a little nervous.

It didn't sound like he was being punished. But it didn't sound good, either.

The principal sighed so loudly that Ray's nerves jumped. Then he cleared his throat. "Ray," he started again. "We've just heard from your home. I'm very sorry to tell you this."

"Tell me what?" Ray asked. He wondered what they were making such a fuss about.

He could feel the silence thicken for a moment. Finally, in a rush, the principal said, "Ray, your mama is dead. Seems she ate something bad, and there was nothing anyone could do. She died last night, before anyone could help her. I'm very, very sorry to tell you this."

Ray didn't say a word. Something had snapped inside him. No one had touched him, but he felt as though he'd been beaten into the ground.

"Ray, can we get you something?" asked the principal, after an uncomfortable silence.

Ray shook his head. He couldn't speak. He could feel a band of steel tightening around his throat. He knew the adults expected him to break down and cry, but he couldn't do it. He just couldn't do anything but feel this thick band pulling tighter and tighter on him.

He didn't say anything, even later that morning, when the principal put him on the train for Greenville.

Ray could smell that special smell in the air when he stepped off the train at Greenville. He'd known that smell all his life. It smelled like home to him, filled with the delicious smells of summer—fresh berries on the vine, fresh watermelon, fresh flowers. He looked forward to that smell whenever he came home. It was the first indication that he was back.

This time, though, Mama wasn't waiting for him at the station. Instead, it was Mary Jane who hugged and held him when he came off the train. "Oh, Ray," she whispered, and he could feel the tears pouring down her cheeks and dripping all over him. "It's so good you're home."

Ray couldn't speak even then. He loved Mary Jane, but home meant Mama, and Mama wasn't here. He was going to stand by as she was buried in a wooden box, and he couldn't do anything about it. His thoughts whirled around and around in his head, but he couldn't put any of them into words. There was a big lump in his throat that wouldn't go away. He couldn't get past it. He couldn't cry. He couldn't do anything but wander around and try to answer politely if someone spoke to him. Mostly, though, he just wanted to be alone.

He didn't sleep at night, and though Mary Jane made him his favorite meals, he couldn't touch them. Something terrible was building up inside him, and he didn't know how to get rid of it.

Mama had died on a Monday night, but the funeral wasn't going to happen until Sunday. The neighbors watched Ray wandering around during that week, wanting to help him, wanting to ease his grief. No one knew what to do.

Finally someone sent for Ma Beck, a very special woman who took care of many of her neighbors when they were sick. Ma Beck was as good as the doctors and much more comforting. She knew about suffering and about life. She'd given birth to twenty-two children, and three of them had died. All her remaining sons and daughters—nineteen of them—adored her as much as the rest of the community.

Ma Beck took one look at Ray and knew that giving him sympathy was hopeless. Nothing would help him get out his pain but some good, hard common sense.

She made sure she was alone with Ray inside Mama's house. Then, instead of talking to him in a hushed whisper and dabbing at her eyes with a handkerchief, as the other women had done, Ma Beck raised her voice and laced into him. "What are you thinkin', boy? You gonna give up now? You gonna turn your back on all those good lessons your mama gave you? You think that's how she'd want to know you turned out? A helpless baby who can't do anything because she's gone? You know she raised you better'n that! Stop actin' crazy, RC. Your mama's dead, and she loved you. And you love her. Now you gotta go on with your life. That's what she always wanted for you."

Ray looked toward the sound of Ma Beck's voice. She was bracing and strong, just like Mama had been. Mama was small and fragile, but in her heart she'd always been a lion, and she'd faced her life with courage. Ray thought of this, and then he dropped his head. The lump that had frozen all his emotions began to dissolve. The tears began to roll down his face.

Ma Beck took him in her arms as though he were a baby and rocked him. Ray cried on and on, howling, screaming, for hours. She whispered to him, telling him it was all right, telling him to get it all out, it would make him feel better.

When he was finally through crying, she insisted he drink several glasses of cool, fresh water from the well. She fixed him a good meal and saw that he ate almost all of it. And when he'd finished, he fell into the bed he and Mama had shared, and dropped into a deep, soundless sleep for the first time in a week.

Mama's funeral drew a large crowd. She'd been a black laundress with almost no education, but there were white people crying at her funeral along with black people. She had been a good and decent woman who'd wanted her sons to live a good life, and many people respected her and would miss her.

Ray walked with the others out to the

graveyard to be present when her coffin was lowered into the ground. Before they closed the lid over Mama's face, he made sure to reach in and cup her cheek in his hand one more time. But the figure lying in the coffin wasn't the real Mama. She was gone somewhere, and Ray understood that she would never come back.

When it was over, Ray left the graveyard along with the other mourners. The week of anguish he'd just lived through had given him a hardness he'd never had before, that he would carry with him for the rest of his life.

"What are you going to do now, boy?" asked some of the neighbors. Ray didn't answer. He was thinking it over. He wouldn't ask advice from anyone; it was too late for that. He was alone now, and he had to make his own decisions.

He thought of Mama's desire for him to be educated. Well, he was educated, as much as he needed. He'd done what she wanted.

Going back to school was pointless. There was nothing more they could teach him that would help him out in the real world.

After a few weeks, Mary Jane, who was still fixing supper for him every night, said quietly, "What are you going to do, Ray? Go back to school in the fall?"

Ray looked up. "No," he said. "I've made up my mind. School can't teach me any more about what I really need to know. It's time for me to get out on my own and work."

"Work at what?"

"Playin' piano, singin'. Anything to do with music."

"You think you can make a livin' doin' that?"

"I been makin' money for years doin' it. It's what I want to do, Mary Jane."

Mary Jane was silent. "You goin' to look for music work around Greensville?" she asked.

"You know I can't," Ray said. He didn't want to sound harsh, not to Mary Jane, whom he loved like a second mother, but now that he'd made the decision, he knew he had to stick by it. If she coddled him, it would just be harder. He swallowed hard and went on. "I got to go to bigger towns. Tallahassee, Tampa. Maybe even Jacksonville. That's where the most work'll be. They'll have lots of clubs there, lots of chances for me to work."

Mary Jane was silent. She'd always hoped he'd stay with her, this boy she looked on as her own son. "When?" she said finally.

"Soon as possible. Tomorrow. Next week. Might as well not put it off, Mary Jane. I ain't got any money, and life ain't gonna be any easier without it. I gotta earn some."

Ray packed his two suits, socks, and underwear. He'd been given a clarinet, which he tucked under his arm. Mary Jane paid for his train ticket to Jacksonville, over a hundred miles away, and gave him the name of some friends he could stay with when he got there.

The day Ray said good-bye to Mary Jane and headed off with his one cardboard suitcase for bigger towns was the beginning of his life as an adult. He had almost no money, and an incomplete education. He was blind, poor, and black. He was alone.

He still felt he could somehow make a living and stand up to anyone.

He was fifteen years old.

# Flopping Around Florida

Mary Jane's friends were named Lena Mae and Fred Thompson. They had a comfortable apartment on Church Street in Jacksonville, and right away they took Ray in and made him feel like one of their own.

They always had hot meals ready for him, and they insisted that he come home by a certain hour, or call if he was delayed. Instead of feeling like he was fighting the world, Ray felt more like part of a family. It made the transition into the adult world a lot easier for him than it might have been, and he was always grateful to them.

The next few months were the toughest Ray had ever known. Aside from the Thompsons, who were always caring and kind, Ray ran into one roadblock after another, trying to get work as a musician.

He heard that going to the union halls would help him secure jobs in the Jacksonville area, so he spent part of each day at the union halls, asking for work, offering to play clarinet, recorder, piano, whatever was needed. He was laughed at, turned away, told to get out of town and let real musicians get on with their work.

Ray persisted. He kept going back to the union halls, trying out whatever he heard on the piano, telling prospective employers to let him play at their club, and if they didn't like what they heard, they didn't have to pay him. He took a number of jobs on that basis, to prove himself and to make a little money.

And though they didn't pay him much, when he finished an evening's work, the club owner always gave him something. It wasn't a fortune, but Ray was managing to earn money every week, and he felt as though, given enough time, he'd break through.

Finally he was able to join his first musician's union, Local Union 632. From then on, he began to be known in the area. Because he was willing to play at any gathering anywhere in the area, he began to be invited to a few jobs. Then he began to get a few more.

Ray quickly learned to ask for his pay, which was always given in cash, in single dollar bills. Otherwise, a promoter or club owner could say he'd been given a five-dollar bill when in fact they'd handed him a one-dollar bill.

"No, thank you," Ray would say when offered a single bill as his evening's pay. "Please pay me in singles, and count them in front of me."

He was on his own now, and he learned quickly that he had to look out for himself.

By the age of sixteen, Ray was eager to

strike out even more on his own. He loved the Thompsons, but he yearned for real independence and a chance to live completely on his own. He decided to go to Orlando.

Orlando was the toughest town of all.

Ray began to wonder whether he wasn't really going to starve to death. Wherever he looked, bands were scratching around for work, and there didn't seem to be any in Orlando. He rented a room from a woman with a big house, but sometimes a couple of days would pass without his being able to eat. When he could scrape together enough for a can of sardines and a box of soda crackers, washed down with a glass of water, it felt like a feast. Sometimes he and a couple of other musicians shared a six-cent bag of beans, which they mixed with some fat, seasoned with salt and pepper, and boiled in a pot.

Finally he met a tenor player who had his own band. Joe Anderson, the tenor player, used regular musical arrangements he bought from a big music house. Ray told him he could do original arrangements, and he made up new arrangements for the songs Joe's band played night after night. Unfortunately he was so excited at being asked to arrange for a big band that he forgot to ask to be paid for it.

Ray still played clarinet, but right now saxophone was the instrument everyone wanted to hear, so Ray taught himself to play alto sax and got a few jobs as a sax player. And eventually he moved to Tampa to try his luck there.

Perhaps the most significant thing that occurred during his time in Tampa was that friends finally convinced Ray to wear dark glasses. His eyes were still tearing up and often had the same filmy goo on them that he'd had in childhood. It didn't look flattering onstage. So Ray got a pair of dark glasses, and from then on he was never without them.

In Tampa, Ray met a guitarist named Gosady McGee, who became a good friend of his. He also met a young girl named Louise and fell in love with her. But Louise's parents weren't thrilled about the idea of a blind and mostly unemployed musician dating their daughter. And one day Ray looked at his life and didn't like what he saw.

He was in his late teens, hardly ever had any money, living in a state where most good musicians didn't live, just visited for a short time. There were no real opportunities for a musician to break into the big time in Florida. The best musicians, he realized, were all from big cities far away, up north.

Ray decided it was time to head out for a bigger place. He told Gosady to come over to the room where he was living and bring a map of the United States.

Puzzled, Gosady showed up with the map. "Okay," Ray said, "now roll that map out so you can see all of the country on it."

Gosady unrolled the map and used the salt and pepper shakers on the table to hold the ends down. "Okay, Ray. What's this about?"

"Gosady," Ray said, "I want you to take a piece of string and put one end on the city of Tampa."

Gosady obeyed. "All right. One end is on Tampa. Now what?"

"Now I want you to pull that string as far as you can and find the city in the U.S. that's farthest away from Tampa. Which is the farthest city you can find that's still an American city?"

Gosady carefully measured with the string. "Well—looks like that would be Seattle."

"Seattle. That in Washington State?"

"Yep. Way northwest, almost in Canada."

Ray thought about it for just a minute. "Okay," he said. "Then that's where I'm goin' next—Seattle."

"You serious?"

"I'm tired of getting nowhere, Gosady. You gotta go somewhere to get somewhere. You wanna come too?"

Gosady thought about it for just a minute.

"Well—sure. Tampa sure is the middle of no-where. Anywhere else has to be better."

"That's what I figured."

So after flopping around Florida, Ray packed his suitcase once again. He had enough money for a bus ticket to Seattle and a burning desire to do better than he'd been doing. It was time for a change of scenery.

He had no way of knowing that in Seattle, his real breakthrough would finally come.

# Seattle

When Ray finally arrived in Seattle, he'd been on a cross-country bus for five days and nights. Gosady was staying behind in Tampa for a while, so Ray had come alone. It had been a miserable trip.

For five days he'd been kept in the back of the bus, in a seat right on top of the bus's motor, which was blowing hot, gassy fumes every minute. Ray could hardly breathe in the choked atmosphere at the back of the bus, and the boredom drove him out of his mind. There was nothing to do but sleep or chew on a candy bar.

Being black, he was not allowed in many of the restaurants and rest stops where the bus let off its passengers for brief periods of time. The food counters he was allowed to eat at offered terrible sandwiches at inflated prices. But he had no choice: He could eat at these miserable places or go hungry until he reached Seattle. Ray chose to eat.

He finally arrived in Seattle at five in the morning. He asked someone standing in the bus station where to find a hotel and got directions to a small place nearby.

Ray made it to the hotel, paid for a room, staggered to the bed, and fell asleep for almost twenty-four hours.

When he woke, it was late at night, and he was hungry and ready to explore his new environment. He called the hotel desk and asked where he could find a place to eat.

"Nothing's open," answered the woman at the desk, sounding puzzled. "It's too late."

Ray thought if he didn't eat something, he

would die of starvation, right then. "There has to be something. Anything."

"Well," she said doubtfully, "there's a club. They serve some food. It's called the Rocking Chair."

"Great!" Ray listened carefully as she gave him directions to the club.

But when he finally got to the Rocking Chair, a big guy was guarding the door. "Can't go in," he muttered to Ray.

"What?" By now, Ray was even hungrier.

"It's Talent Night. And you're too young to be here."

"But I'm a musician!"

"Says you."

"I am—let me in, I'll play!"

Ray was never sure whether it was because he was eager or desperately hungry, but he prevailed on the bouncer to let him into the club. And after he sat down at the piano and belted out some of his favorite blues tunes, singing along with the piano, a man came

138

up and offered him a job for a trio—three musicians—if he'd come to the Elks Club on Friday night. By now it was around 6 a.m. on Wednesday.

Ray, excited, said he certainly could have a trio together by Friday. They'd be there Friday night.

He'd been in Seattle for about a day, and awake for about two hours. Already it seemed like Seattle would be a good town for him.

When Ray's friend Gosady McGee arrived in town, he and a bassist named Milt Garred formed a permanent trio. They called themselves the McSon Trio, for the first two letters of Gosady's last name and the last three letters of Ray's.

However, Ray was getting more and more uncomfortable with questions people asked him about his name. It was his real name, but there was also a famous boxer named Sugar Ray Robinson, and sometimes people confused them. Though Ray would never have considered getting into a boxing ring, he decided he wanted his own unique name, something no one would mistake for someone else.

He decided to drop his last name, Robinson, and use his first and middle names. From then on he was known as Ray Charles.

Around this time he also met a talented teenager who would become a lifelong friend. His name was Quincy Jones, and he played the trumpet and wrote jazz. Eventually, he, like Ray, would become an important name in the music business. Quincy was one of Ray's first close friends in the music business, and they would remain friends for the rest of Ray's life.

The cool Seattle weather and continual rain spurred Ray's interest in writing songs. He'd written a few before, but one of the first he wrote in Seattle was a blues song called "The Snow Is Falling." Seattle isn't a city that usually gets snow, but for a southern boy, it must have seemed just as cold and bleak as a blizzard at times.

The McSon Trio specialized in the blues music Ray had been raised on. With Ray on piano, Gosady on guitar, and Milt on bass, they were booked at the Rocking Chair, where they played from one to five a.m. almost every night. Ray also did extra work arranging songs for bands around town.

In a few months the McSon Trio was being asked to work in various towns around Seattle—Tacoma, Kirkland, and Fort Lawton—in addition to playing their regular gig at the Rocking Chair. Soon they were asked to appear on the radio. The trio agreed as long as they could give out Gosady's phone number, so they might get some more bookings.

The radio show was successful enough for Ray and the trio to be offered a chance to do their own live television show, which lasted about six weeks in the Seattle area. Then they were offered the chance to record some

songs for a record label called Downbeat.

This meant the group was really becoming more than just one of the many local bands. They were important enough that a record producer wanted to make their records and sell them all over the country. It was definitely the start of the big time.

The trio recorded two songs in their first session: one that Ray had written in Florida, called "Confession Blues," and the other written by one of his school friends, called "I Love You, I Love You."

A few months later Ray went down to Los Angeles, where Downbeat's offices were located, and recorded more of his own songs, without the trio. The first was called "Baby, Let Me Hold Your Hand." It was Ray's first solo-recorded song and the first to become a national hit. Within a few years it had sold a hundred thousand copies.

Ray decided it was time to move to Los Angeles, where the heart of the recording business was. He thought there would be more opportunities for him and more good musicians and producers he could connect with.

He moved down to L.A. at the age of eighteen.

Gosady and Milt came down too, but they didn't stay very long. They recorded some songs with Ray, but there just weren't many chances for a trio in a big city with so many musicians already established. They decided to go back to Seattle. Ray stayed in L.A.

In the spring of 1950, Ray went out touring on the road with a band for the first time. From then on he'd spend little time at home, even though he eventually had a family. Musicians toured so they could be seen and become known. They toured because it paid well and because it offered them the chance to be in the company of other great musicians.

It was a way of life Ray would live for almost thirty years.

# Taking a Stand

Being on the road had its own routine. Most of the bands Ray worked with traveled by bus from town to town, checking into hotels near the halls where they played. They would rest, take care of their laundry, and then go to a rehearsal, where they'd see the hall, the bandstand, and what they had in the way of lights and sound equipment. They'd run over the songs they'd be doing in their set that night. When rehearsal was over, they would eat an early dinner and change into their suits and starched shirts and ties for the performance.

After the show was over, they'd go out or play cards to wind down. They would go to sleep around dawn, sleep till late morning or early afternoon, and get up to start all over again.

Within a few months of joining his first band, run by Lowell Fulson, a blues guitarist, Ray had taken charge of the band and was running rehearsals, as well as writing the band's arrangements, contributing his own songs, playing sax and piano, and singing. Before, he had worked hard at trying to sound like Nat "King" Cole and Charles Brown, two famous singers. He loved it when people said he sounded just like them.

Suddenly, Ray began to think about being more of an individual to the audiences he played for. He began to think it was more important to develop his own sound that people could identify with him alone. As good as he was at imitating others, he knew now that he had to work at creating his own style.

Life was busy, hectic, and fun for the still-teenaged Ray Charles. But as the bands toured larger and larger areas of the country, he began to see that the divisions between black people and white people were not something he'd left behind when he left Florida. To one degree or another, depending on what part of the country he was in, it was still there. Black people were considered inferior to whites. They had fewer job opportunities than white people, even if they were just as qualified. They were banned from many restaurants, nightclubs, and hotels. In the South, especially, they were treated with disdain at best and often could get only the most menial, low-paying jobs. Once, in Myrtle Beach, South Carolina, when Ray went swimming on an off-day with some of the musicians, they called him back frantically and told him he had almost swum into the "white side" of the ocean. He had to stay on the black side, they told him. Ray thought that was just silly. How could you divide an ocean?

Ray thought little about this prejudice for a long time. He was too busy establishing his career, writing songs and arrangements, touring, and recording. He thought more about going out on his own, starting his own band, and bringing in girl backup singers who would sing his songs with him on the bandstand.

Within just a few years, he had done all those things. The Ray Charles Band became a fixture on the road, touring almost fifty weeks a year, and the Raeletts, his girl backup singers, sang Ray's hits with him, night after night, and on his records. Of course, virtually every musician he worked with was black, as were the girl singers. They were talented and he liked working with them. But from one moment to the next, Ray's eyes were opened to the full extent of the unfairness that black people faced every day in their lives.

By 1961, Ray had been on the road for more than ten years. He was writing songs and arrangements, playing piano and sax, and working with

the Raeletts when they weren't recording in Los Angeles.

Now, though, he had a concert date in Georgia. The big bus with Ray's name on it swung into the parking lot near the concert hall. Ray was met by the concert promoter, who set up the concert dates and made sure they ran smoothly.

The promoter told Ray that there was a problem. They needed to be sure that the white audience sat close to the stage and that the black people sat far away, in the balcony. That's the way it always was, especially in the South.

For Ray, that didn't make sense, even though he knew why the promoter was insisting on it. Black people had been Ray's best audience for his entire career. They'd come to the clubs to hear him, bought his records, spread his fame. He felt he owed them more than the white audience.

Ray told the promoter that he understood

that blacks and whites had to be separated here in Georgia. How about putting the black audience in front and the white people up in the balcony? That would be a fairer arrangement, and one he could live with.

The promoter refused. This was Georgia, he insisted, and in Georgia, the white people always got the best seats.

Ray took a deep breath. He'd gone along, for years, with bad hotels, bad food, with sitting in the back of the bus. He'd put up with being banned from clubs and restaurants because of his skin color. He'd finally reached the moment when he wouldn't put up with it anymore.

"No," he said to the promoter. "If you don't let the black people sit close to the stage where they belong, we won't play here."

The promoter gasped as though he'd been punched in the stomach. "What are you saying? We're completely booked—there are hundreds of people coming here to see you!"

"That's too bad. I owe my audience some- thing. They've been good to me, and I have to look out for them."

"If you don't play," the promoter said coldly, "I'll take you to court and sue you. I'll make sure you never play in this state again."

"You can do what you want," Ray said calmly. "But if black people don't sit in the best seats, my band won't play here."

Ray kept his word. He didn't play the date in Georgia. The promoter kept his word too. He took Ray to court. Ray tried to explain to the judge that he was just looking out for the people who'd been most loyal to him, but the judge didn't care. All he saw was the state law that said blacks and whites had to be sepa- rated was being challenged by this musician. He ordered Ray to pay the promoter back the money he owed and to pay for his legal costs as well.

Ray didn't play in Georgia again for years.

Now that he began to see what was really

happening between the races, Ray looked around at what others were doing about it. He saw other black people who were angered by the injustices and wanting to change things.

After looking at all the leaders stepping forward to be heard, Ray decided he would follow Dr. Martin Luther King Jr., who was advocating change through peaceful, non-violent methods. Ray thought Dr. King had the right idea and that, given enough time, his methods would work.

They did work. Ray joined the movement to help out. He knew he could not participate with Dr. King in his civil rights marches. Being blind, Ray would not know if someone was throwing a brick or a bottle at him until it was too late. But Ray worked behind the scenes to raise money to help Dr. King change the system.

Slowly things began to change. Schools began to integrate. Buses no longer insisted that black people ride in back. Hearts and

153

minds began to open. Ray felt satisfied that he was a part of this great change.

Many years later, in 1979, Ray was invited to the Georgia statehouse. The governor told him that, all those years ago, Ray had been right and the law had been wrong. But that law was gone now, and things were better. The ceremony ended when Ray sang one of his biggest hits, "Georgia on My Mind." He was given a standing ovation.

# A Grand Life

Ray continued to be an enormous influence on the music scene for the rest of his life.

Eventually, after almost thirty years, he stopped touring and began to focus on recording so more people could enjoy his work even if he couldn't play for them live.

He went from recording with Swingtime Records to recording at Atlantic Records, and then to ABC Records. Many of his songs became huge hits, including "Hit the Road, Jack," "What'd I Say," and "I Got a Woman." Unlike other recording artists, Ray played and sang not only rhythm and blues, but also popular songs, jazz, rock 'n' roll, and other styles. He recorded duets with famous singers. He made a recording of George Gershwin's landmark folk opera *Porgy and Bess*. He wrote and recorded hundreds of his own songs.

Finally, in 1962, Ray set his sights on a new dream: building his own recording studio. He wanted a place that would belong to him, where no one else would record, and where he could feel comfortable coming to an office every day.

He developed a record label of his own, Tangerine Records (named after his favorite fruit), and recorded many hits through his own label. The construction of his recording studio in Los Angeles, RPM International, was begun in 1962 and finished in early 1964. It became his professional home for the rest of his life.

Now when Ray went on the road, he went on shorter trips but to faraway places:

He played in Europe. He played in Israel. He played all over the world, to screaming, enthusiastic audiences. Because he played so many different styles of music, he attracted more and more people of all ages, sexes, and races as fans.

As he got older, he found new challenges to conquer. He appeared in a couple of movies, including *The Blues Brothers*, starring John Belushi and Dan Aykroyd. He did commercials, playing his music on television and talking to the camera. In 1985, he joined dozens of top recording artists to sing "We Are the World," a record made and sold to benefit world hunger relief.

He also found time to marry twice. He had twelve children and eighteen grandchildren.

He became an excellent chess player. He won often, because he could memorize the moves on the chessboard.

In 1993, he played "America the Beautiful" at the inaugural ball of President Bill Clinton, who had been his fan since childhood. From growing up in a poor, backwoods town to playing in front of the president of the United States was a long journey. Ray took that journey with nothing but his talent, determination, and desire for independence.

He was especially delighted when movie director Taylor Hackford, a lifelong fan, asked if he could make a film about Ray's life. It took a number of years to bring *Ray* to the screen, but Ray himself read many drafts of the script and offered suggestions and corrections, and he also helped audition Jamie Foxx, who eventually played him in the film.

Ray became ill in 2004. He knew he wasn't going to live very long. Still, he kept going to his studio, working on new recordings, and staying involved with his friends and his family.

In his last public appearance, he came, weak but smiling, to see his recording studio, RPM, dedicated as a historic landmark in Los Angeles. Many fans showed up to see him and roared at the sight of him. Ray nodded back to them. He'd given them all of himself through his music. They in turn called him "Brother Ray," an affectionate nickname he'd carried from the time he first became famous. It was a wonderful day for everyone to see his studio, the apex of his dreams, marked as an important place in a city as large as Los Angeles.

Ray died on June 10, 2004, at the age of seventy-three.

The following year, the United States Post Office, which had previously put his likeness on a stamp, honored him further by renaming its station on West Adams Street in Los Angeles. That post office would be known from then on as the Ray Charles Station.

Also, in 2005, Jamie Foxx became the second black actor to win an Oscar for Best Actor. He won it for playing Ray Charles.

One has to think that Ray would have been proud.

# For More Information

## BOOKS

Beyer, Mark. *Rock & Roll Hall of Famers: Ray Charles*. New York: Rosen Central, 2002.

Charles, Ray, and David Ritz. *Brother Ray: Ray Charles' Own Story*. New York: Da Capo Press, 1978; expanded version 2004.

Lydon, Michael. *Ray Charles: Man and Music*. New York: Routledge, 2004.

Mathis, Sharon Bell. *Ray Charles*. New York: Lee & Low Books, 1973 text copyright renewed 2001.

Ritz, David. *Ray Charles: Voice of Soul*. New York: Chelsea House Publishers, 1994.

Turk, Ruth. *Ray Charles: Soul Man*. Minneapolis: Lerner Publications Company, 1996.

White, James L. *RAY: A Tribute to the Movie, the Music, and the Man*. US: Newmarket Press, 2004.

## FILMS

*Ray* (DVD). Directed by Taylor Hackford; screenplay by James L. White from a story by Taylor Hackford and James L. White; released by Universal Pictures, 2004.

## WEBSITES

www.RayCharles.com

## ★★★ Childhood of Famous Americans ★★★

One of the most popular series ever published for young Americans, these classics have been praised alike by parents, teachers, and librarians. With these lively, inspiring, fictionalized biographies—easily read by children of eight and up—today's youngster is swept right into history.

## ★★★ Collect them all! ★★★

# CHILDHOOD OF WORLD FIGURES

CHRISTOPHER COLUMBUS

ANNE FRANK

DIANA, PRINCESS OF WALES

POPE JOHN PAUL II

LEONARDO DA VINCI

MOTHER TERESA

GANDHI

THE BUDDHA

COMING SOON:

MARIE CURIE

★ ★ COLLECT THEM ALL! ★ ★